# 3.7

Bella Baxter #5

# Bella Baxter
## and the
# Lighthouse
# Mystery

# Read all of
# Bella Baxter's adventures:

ALADDIN PAPERBACKS

Published by Simon & Schuster

xter #3

# Bella Baxter
# and the
# Lighthouse
# Mystery

### Jane B. Mason & Sarah Hines Stephens
### Illustrated by John Shelley

Aladdin Paperbacks
New York  London  Toronto  Sydney

*To Nora, a chicken crazy girl—*
*J. B. M and S. H. S*

ALADDIN PAPERBACKS
An imprint of Simon & Schuster Children's Publishing Division
1230 Avenue of the Americas, New York, NY 10020
Text copyright © 2006 by Jane B. Mason and Sarah Hines Stephens
Illustrations copyright © 2006 by John Shelley
All rights reserved, including the right of reproduction in whole or
in part in any form.
ALADDIN PAPERBACKS and colophon are trademarks
of Simon & Schuster, Inc.
Designed by Debra Sfetsios
The text of this book was set in Baskerville.
Manufactured in the United States of America
First Aladdin Paperbacks edition April 2006
2  4  6  8  10  9  7  5  3  1
Library of Congress Control Number 2005926075
ISBN-13: 978-0-689-86282-3
ISBN-10: 0-689-86282-2

# Bella Baxter #3

## Bella Baxter
and the
# Lighthouse
# Mystery

CHAPTER 1

# Lotsa Lava

"Bella?"

Bella jerked awake and spilled her popcorn. It went all over the couch and the floor. She rubbed her eyes. The fuzzy television screen came into view. Shocking. She'd fallen asleep while watching a documentary. It was by one of her favorite moviemakers, Mason Hawk.

It was shocking because (1) Bella loved documentaries. They were like great stories—only better because they were true! And (2) *Lotsa Lava: Volcanic Eruptions of the Last Decade* was amazing. It was almost as good as Mason Hawk's best

film, *Deep-Sea Divers: Submarines In Depth*. Bella had watched that one seven times. Without yawning! She must have been tired to fall asleep during *Lotsa Lava*. Really, really tired.

At least she wasn't the only one. Bella's dad stretched and let out a big yawn. "Time for bed, pudding head," he said. He tousled his daughter's hair. "We've got a big day tomorrow."

All of a sudden Bella felt wide-awake. She had some fast-talking to do. She couldn't go to sleep now. She had to see the rest of the film tonight.

*Lotsa Lava* was the only Mason Hawk movie she hadn't seen. And Mason Hawk was coming to stay at Sea Inn. In less than twelve hours!

Mason wasn't the first fabulous guest to come to stay. But he *was* the most famous. At least so far.

"But, Dad!" Bella protested. "I've got to see the end! Mason Hawk will be here in the morning. I need to be ready!" She opened her eyes really wide and stuck out her lower lip. It was her best puppy dog face. But she couldn't tell if it was working.

Barnaby shook his head. He pointed to the stairs. "Bella, it's after ten. You can watch it later. Right now you need to scoot up to bed."

"But—"

"Right now," Barnaby said, giving her his "I mean business" look. He didn't use that look very often. Bella knew better than to argue when he did. Bella *had* to go to bed. But she didn't have to like it.

Bella heaved a giant sigh. Then she picked up

every single piece of popcorn. S-l-o-w-l-y. At first her dad looked like he was trying not to laugh. Then his hands moved to his hips. Bella set the popcorn bowl on the coffee table and headed for the stairs. Two minutes later she was brushing her teeth. She stared straight into the bathroom mirror.

"Hello, Mr. Hawk," she said smoothly through a mouthful of toothpaste. "I'm Bella, your biggest fan." She smiled widely at her reflection. Toothpaste foam dribbled down her chin. Bella had to laugh. The foamy beard was not very charming.

Bella went into her room. She pulled on her pajamas and climbed into bed. With her head on two pillows she could see out her window. She liked to look at the stars before she fell asleep. But tonight the fog was so thick she couldn't see the stars *or* the moon. The sky was a glowing gray. It was almost . . . spooky.

Bella shivered in her cool sheets. She pulled the covers up to her chin. She loved living near the ocean. But it sure was different from living in

Hartford. Hartford was smack-dab in the middle of Connecticut. There wasn't a body of water in sight. Here in Sandyport the ocean was everywhere. Even in the air.

Bella listened. When the house was quiet, she could hear the sound of waves lapping on the shore. *Lap. Lap. Lap.* And then a muffled *Ka-boom* when a big wave crashed on the beach. The constant sound lulled her to sleep.

Her eyes were starting to close when a light appeared through her window. It moved quickly across the wall, her floor, and her bed. Then it disappeared.

*That's weird*, Bella thought. She was drifting off to sleep. It couldn't be car headlights on the ocean side of the house. So what was it? Bella was curious. But a moment later she was completely asleep.

# CHAPTER 2

# A Strange Feeling

Bella set a large stack of plates on the buffet. Then she headed back into the kitchen for pastries and fruit. After bringing out the food, she set out the juice glasses and silverware. Then she quickly folded the napkins into neat triangles that stood on their own. She could fold napkin angels and turkeys, too. But triangles were best for every day. Besides, they were the quickest to fold.

Bella was not a fast enough talker to convince her dad to let her stay up the night before. But she *was* a fast thinker and a fast enough worker to solve her problem. None of the Sea Inn guests had come down yet. Her breakfast tasks were already done. Bella would have just enough time to finish her movie before she had to clean up.

Bella slipped into the study. She found the spot in the film where she had dozed off. And she punched a button on the remote control. Minutes later she was engrossed in the second half of *Lotsa Lava*. "Chance's Peak in Montserrat bubbled over like a massive pot of scalding tomato soup," Mason Hawk said. The huge mountain on the screen spewed a fountain of simmering red lava. "Within minutes the molten

lava had covered everything in its path, burning it to cinders or burying it forever." The molten stuff oozed on-screen, slow but unstoppable.

Bella's eyes widened. This was totally cool! She must have been really wiped out last night.

"Great building," the narrator's voice continued. Bella blinked. There was no building on the television screen. What was Mr. Hawk talking about? Had he messed up his own film?

"Has it been in your family for long?" the voice went on.

"Thank you. And no. We won it in an online contest. We've been working hard to restore it ever since."

Hang on. Bella knew both of those voices. And her mom wasn't in the habit of narrating documentaries. She hit the remote again and the movie stopped.

The narrator was talking to Bella's mom! Mason Hawk was here—early, and in the flesh!

Bella streaked into the hall where Sea Inn's guests checked in. She lurched to a halt. Sure enough, there was Mason Hawk! He was surrounded by three rumpled-looking people dressed in lots of black—two men and one woman.

Mason looked cool in jeans and a vest with lots of pockets. The others looked hot. They had heavy bags slung over their shoulders. And they had black circles under their eyes. They must be Mason's crew.

Bella stood staring. She took it all in with her mouth half-open. She'd practiced her introduction the night before (after she'd brushed and spit). But now she felt . . . strange. Her palms were a little sweaty. Her stomach was a little fluttery. For the first time in her life Bella Baxter felt shy!

"This is my daughter, Bella," Bella's mother said.

Bella looked up at Mason. She wanted to say something. Unfortunately, her tongue felt as dry as sandpaper.

"Bell, can you take these folks up to their rooms?" Nellie asked.

Bella nodded mutely. She led the way up the stairs and down the hall. She pointed out Vista and Wave Crest to the crew. Then she opened the door to Seascape for Mason. She had picked out Seascape herself. It was her favorite room. "This is your home away from home, Mr. Hawk," she said with a nervous gulp. She wiped her hands on her jeans. Mason Hawk was even cooler in person than he was in his films.

"Call me Mason," he replied. He ran a hand through his messy dark hair. "And how'd you know my name?"

"I'm a huge fan," Bella blurted. "Maybe your biggest."

"Really?" Mason said. "You've seen my films?"

"Of course. I just watched *Lotsa Lava* last night. I liked it. It was even better than *Twisting Tornadoes* and *Hurricane Havoc*. But I think *Deep-Sea Divers* is my favorite."

"*Deep-Sea Divers* is one of my favorites too," Mason agreed with a nod. Then he sighed. "Too bad the critics can't see it for the film it is."

"Maybe the critics just aren't that . . . deep," Bella said. She smirked. *Would he get the joke?*

Mason snorted and gave Bella a huge smile in return. Bella's mouth turned up in a grin. She'd made him laugh! She, Bella Baxter, had made Mason Hawk laugh! Then her smile suddenly disappeared. The funny shy feeling returned.

She swallowed hard and took a deep breath. Bella had wanted to ask Mason a question since she'd found out he was coming to Sea Inn. This was her chance. "So, uh, are you just on vacation? Or are you going to make a movie about Sandyport?"

"Well, I don't usually like to talk about my upcoming projects." Mason looked very serious. "But since you're such a big fan, I'll tell you." His smile came back. "I'm working on a movie about East Coast lighthouses. There are lots right around here."

"Cool!" Bella exclaimed. Then she remembered something. "We've got a lighthouse right down the shore! They don't use it anymore, but

I can take you there if you want. I'm practically an expert on it." That last part wasn't exactly true. But Bella figured that with her connections she could become an expert in a jiffy.

Mason nodded slowly. "Okay, you've got a deal. And a date. How about later this afternoon? Say around two o'clock?"

Bella was so excited she wanted to hop up and down. But she had to be cool. "Sure, sounds great," she said. She waved good-bye and headed downstairs. Luckily the other Sea Inn guests were done with breakfast. She quickly cleared the buffet and the table.

"I'm going to the library!" she told her mom as she handed over the last load of dirty plates in the kitchen.

"Okay, sweetie," her mom replied.

Bella dashed up to her room and grabbed her backpack and library card. Then she raced out the door. She had a lot of lighthouse research to do. She had to become an expert by two o'clock!

# CHAPTER 3

# Lotsa Lighthouses

Bella thumbed through a copy of *Off the Rocks: A History of Lighthouses*. The pages were yellowed and water stained. But the text was still fascinating. The very first lighthouses were built in Egypt and Greece. The stone towers had real fires burning at the top! Lighthouses had been in use for thousands of years. And the Statue of Liberty was the first American lighthouse with an electric light.

Bella closed the heavy book and set it aside. She wished she had a month to read about lighthouses. There was so much to know! The stack of 387.1s sitting in front of her stood higher than her head. There were ten heavy books in the pile. Several of them focused on East Coast lighthouses.

*Whump!* Make that eleven.

"There," Bella's friend Trudy said. The librarian sounded a little breathless. She dusted off her hands and pushed her cat-eye glasses back up her nose. "I think that's all of them. Or all of the good ones, at least."

"Thanks, Trudy," Bella said gratefully. She could always count on Trudy and her library for help and information. Not to mention her gung ho attitude about almost anything.

"No problem, *ma chérie*," Trudy said. "Besides, I owe you for finding a home for my baby chicks. Did you ask your parents about letting us use that old coop behind your house?"

Bella shook her head. "I've been so excited about Mason Hawk coming to stay that I forgot. I'll ask them soon, I promise."

Trudy nodded and picked up the book on the top of the stack. It was called *Piercing the Dark:*

*Lighthouses Then and Now.* "Lighthouses are one of my favorite subjects." She pushed the stack of books aside. Then she pulled out a chair and sat down across from Bella. Finally she looked around to make sure no one was nearby.

"You've heard the legend of the Sandyport lighthouse, haven't you?" she whispered.

Bella shook her head and dropped the copy of *You Light Up My Lighthouse* to her lap. She loved it when Trudy had some extra information to share. And she usually did!

"This isn't in any of the books, mind you. This is local legend. Not only is our little lighthouse one of the oldest around, it's . . ."—Trudy paused and leaned in closer—"haunted."

Bella leaned in too, to hear better. "Haunted?" she repeated. "By who?"

"By the ghost of Elijah 'Salty' Dobin, that's who," Trudy said in her regular library voice. "He was the lighthouse keeper for more than thirty years. He lived and breathed the sea and that lighthouse. He was always there to guide the ships through any kind of storm. And then, one day about ten years ago, he disappeared. Poof! Just like that." Trudy sat up and waved her arms like a magician.

Bella gulped for the second time that day. "Disappeared?" she said.

Trudy nodded, her face dead serious. "Disappeared." She brushed her hands together and shook her head a little sadly. "The lighthouse hasn't been used since. It's not really needed anymore. These days ships have all kinds of new technology to keep them from running aground."

Bella picked up a new book, one called *Guiding Lights: Lighthouses of the Eastern Seaboard*.

"But that's not the end of the story," Trudy said. She leaned forward again. "For years afterward sailors swore that light still shone from our shore on stormy, foggy nights. They say Salty is still in that lighthouse, protecting and guiding ships."

Bella stared at Trudy. Part of her hoped her friend was kidding. The other part wanted all of this to be true. The question was, which part was bigger?

"Excuse me," said a voice.

Bella jumped. All this talk about ghosts had her spooked. She looked up and saw a man standing next to their table. He wasn't Salty. But he was dirty. His entire torso was covered in muddy paw prints.

The man looked at Trudy. He had a desperate expression on his face. "Can you tell me where I can find some books on dog training?" he asked.

"Sure thing," Trudy said. She got to her feet and led the man toward the 636.7s.

Bella watched the two make their way through the stacks. Then she opened *Guiding Lights* and stared. There were 540 pages in the book. And she'd opened to the one with a picture of the Sandyport lighthouse. In front of the lighthouse stood a smiling man with a long gray beard. Salty Dobin!

Bella suddenly remembered the light that had flashed across her bed the night before. It had not come from a car. She shuddered. It had come from the lighthouse!

CHAPTER 4

# Lighthouse Lore

Bella slung her book-laden backpack over her shoulder. Ugh. It was heavy. Bella waved good-bye to Trudy. She wanted to stay longer at the library and learn more about the Sandyport lighthouse. But it was already one thirty. Time to head back to the inn and meet Mason. Thank goodness she was a quick study. She'd be getting by with what she'd learned from reading for three hours! And from Trudy, of course.

Bella was not planning to tell Mason about Salty. She didn't want to freak him out on his first day in Sandyport. Besides, there were lots of other things she could tell him about her new favorite subject. Things that were a lot less spooky.

Bella made it home in a record six minutes. She didn't want to keep Mason waiting. She hurried up the steps to Sea Inn's big wraparound porch. But when she rounded a corner, she ran right into one of Mason's crew. He wore a long stocking cap over his dreadlocks, and a tie-dyed shirt—black and gray.

"Whoa," he said as Bella crashed into him. Her heavy pack banged against her back. He pulled off his hat and headphones and stuck a finger in his ringing ear. "I thought you were a stampede of elephants."

He put the headphones back on and yelled over his shoulder. "The mike is working, Darla," he reported. "Can you turn it down?"

A blond girl with long braids and a bandanna walked up behind him. "Check that, Sterling." She nodded and pulled off her own headphones.

"Sorry, Sterling," Bella said. What a cool name! "Are you filming here?"

Sterling shook his head. "We're j
equipment. Have to make sure it n
okay."

"Right." Bella nodded. Part of her
stay and find out more. But she had an appoint-
ment to keep. Plus she was hoping to get one
more glance at the books in her pack. So she said
good-bye and headed into the kitchen.

Inside, her mother was finishing tea sandwiches. Bella grabbed a cutoff crust and made
for the front hall. Her dad was talking to the
third crewmember. Bella heard her father ask
about a wheeled contraption that was set up on
the throw rug. Bella guessed it was a special kind
of camera holder.

"Wow!" Barnaby said. "How does it work,
Lyle?"

Bella smiled to herself. Should she tell Lyle
that her dad was as klutzy as he was curious?

Too late. Before Bella could say anything, her
dad reached out to turn a knob. He stumbled
on the edge of the rug and knocked into the

uipment. A second later the camera holder lay in a heap on the floor.

"I'm so sorry!" Barnaby said. He bent down alongside Lyle. He was carefully examining the fallen contraption.

"That's okay, man," Lyle said.

Just then Mason appeared at the top of the stairs. He carried a black satchel over his shoulder and smiled when he spotted Bella.

"Ready to go?" he asked.

Oh, well. Bella slipped her book-stuffed backpack onto a hook in the foyer. She obviously wouldn't have time for a final peek at her books. She'd have to go on what she knew already.

"Absolutely!" she said with a grin.

Nellie Baxter appeared with a paper bag. "Some sandwiches and juice for sustenance," she said. Bella took the bag gratefully. She was starving.

"Thanks, Mom," she said. "See you all later."

Barnaby looked up from his spot on the floor. "Where are you going, Bellisimo?" he asked.

"I'm just going to show Mason a few things,"

Bella said over her shoulder. She didn't want to explain too much to her dad. If she did, he might invite himself along. And she wanted to have Mason all to herself. Even if it was a little bit selfish.

Bella led Mason out the front door and down the steps. It was just before two, but the fog was already rolling in. You could barely see the ocean, even from the cliff path.

Bella zipped up her sweatshirt. She led the way down the rocky trail to the lighthouse. It was time to get busy talking. She had a lot to tell Mason if she was going to brief him on the lighthouse before they got there.

"Our lighthouse is more than two hundred years old," Bella said proudly. "It's one hundred and forty-two feet high. The sandstone at the base comes from a quarry in Vermont. They moved it to Sandyport by dogsled! The lighthouse and cottage beneath it took three years to build. It has been functional since 1788. It's closed now, of course. It hasn't been used since the last keeper, Elijah Dobin, uh, left. That was about ten years ago." *At least it hasn't been used officially.* Bella heard Trudy's voice echo in her head. "But folks say the light still works," she finished aloud.

They came around a bend, and Bella strained to see the lighthouse on the point. Its chipping blue and red paint was barely visible through the fog.

"The lighthouse tower is painted red for overall visibility during daylight hours," Bella explained. "But at night it's the lighthouse's light that pierces the dark and keeps the ships off the rocks. The original light had twenty oil blazes. They were merged into a single light with mirrors and lenses. The current light features a Fresnel lens, which was invented by Frenchman Augustin Fresnel in 1822. And we have a sound siren, too."

Bella thought she sounded just like a documentary narrator. But as they got closer, she trailed off. Through the fog something up in the tower caught her eye.

Was there a light in the window? Was Salty there *right now*? Bella shivered and pulled her sweatshirt hood strings. Mason wasn't saying much. For a moment Bella considered telling him about Salty's legend. But what if he felt as spooked as she did right now? What if he packed up and left town?

# CHAPTER 5

# Do Not Enter

"Here we are," Bella announced.

Mason still wasn't talking. He squinted through the fog toward the top of the lighthouse. Every once in a while he rubbed his hands together.

"But it looks like this is as far as we can go." Bella gestured toward the board nailed over the front door of the cottage. DO NOT ENTER was sloppily painted across it in red paint. She tried to sound disappointed, but secretly she was relieved. Maybe she could just take Mason to the library. It might be best to leave Salty undisturbed.

"See, it's locked." Bella reached past the board

and tried the rusted door handle. It turned with a screech that made her jump. Mason reached over and pushed on the peeling blue door. It opened a crack. Then a huge gust of wind pushed the door the rest of the way open with a bang.

At least Bella hoped it was the wind.

"Brilliant!" Mason finally spoke. He ducked right under the barrier and headed inside. "Can we get up in the tower?"

"Oh. Um. Probably." Bella followed Mason inside but left the door standing open. They might need to make a hasty exit.

"It's a little creepy in here, isn't it?" Mason said. He sounded delighted.

All Bella could do was nod. It was more than a little creepy. It was a lot creepy. For one thing, the fog made it seem later in the afternoon than it was. And the cottage was not empty. It was crowded with furniture and bits and parts of old ships. It looked like Salty had left in a hurry. Or like he hadn't left at all.

Holding his fingers in facing *L*s, Mason peered around the cottage. He gazed at different windows, walls, and nooks. Bella watched him and tried not to shiver. She wrapped her arms around herself to keep out the damp wind and the creeps. She thought she heard Mason mumble something about the light. There sure wasn't a lot of it in here.

Bella squinted through the gloom and took a closer look around.

There was a lot of sailing stuff—anchors, fishing nets, a giant steering wheel, pieces of cloth, pulleys, coiled ropes. An old radio sat on a dusty shelf. The small sofa was covered with tattered cushions. There was a tiny kitchen, too. A teakettle and cup sat on a table. A chair beside the table was pushed back just a little—like somebody had gotten up to answer the door. Bella took a step closer and peered into the cup. She saw something strange—a last gulp of tea. It looked like somebody had gotten up to answer the door just a few minutes ago!

This was getting spookier by the minute. Suddenly Bella was very aware that Mason had wandered into the next room. She was all alone! She hurried into a small bedroom. Right away she spotted a neatly made bed. A navy sailor's cap hung on the wall. Mason already had his head inside a small door.

"This must be the stairway to the tower." His

voice echoed. "Wow. This place is even better than I'd thought!" Mason started up. His boots clomped loudly on the wooden stairs.

Bella poked her own head inside the little doorway. It was dark. She tried the light switch. It didn't work. Usually Bella thought of herself as pretty brave. But she did *not* want to meet Salty's ghost in a dark stairway. And she didn't want to hang out downstairs alone, either. Bella tried not to shudder. She grasped the handrail. She put one sneaker on the first step, and stopped.

Over the echoing thumps of Mason's heavy boot steps Bella heard another noise: a second set of footsteps. They were lighter and came from farther up the tower.

Bella raced as fast as she could up the winding stairs. She ignored the dark. She grabbed Mason's coat as soon as she was close enough, and tugged. "There's something I forgot to tell you," she whispered urgently. "We've got to get out of here—now!"

"What is it?" Mason asked. He did not budge from his step.

"Shhh." Bella shushed him. "I'll tell you outside. Hurry." Bella pulled a reluctant Mason by his coat down the stairs and through the two cottage rooms. Finally they were out into the fog. But she did not stop until they were on the other side of the first dune. Then she collapsed in a heap and tried to catch her breath.

"Are you going to tell me what's going on?" Mason put his hands on his hips. But the look on his face was not an angry one. He looked like he had just heard a bad joke.

"It's him," Bella panted. "The ghost of Salty. He's in there!"

"You mean this lighthouse is haunted?"

"That's what I mean." Bella flopped her head back on the sand. She told Mason everything she knew. While she talked, Mason kept looking at the tower and nodding. He didn't laugh. For a long time he didn't even smile.

"Haunted," Mason repeated to himself.

"So I guess we'd better get back to the inn." Bella stood up and brushed herself off.

"Leave?" Mason's serious look disappeared. He began rubbing his hands together again. The corners of his eyes crinkled up mischievously. "I'm not going anywhere but back inside!"

# CHAPTER 6

# Something Brewing

Bella watched Mason duck under the board nailed across the lighthouse door. In an instant he disappeared back inside. He was gone before she could stop him. But there was no way she was going to follow him. Not with Salty still in there.

"I'll wait for you out here!" Bella yelled. She didn't think Mason could hear her over the sound of the surf. "It's not so creepy out here," Bella said more quietly.

But it wasn't so *un*-creepy, either. The wind was picking up. The fog felt like it was soaking through her sweatshirt. Bella kept one fist stuffed in her pocket. In the other one she still had the paper bag her mom had given her. Lunch!

Bella opened the bag and took out two small sandwiches wrapped in wax paper. She left four for Mason and sat down to eat. In only eight bites the sandwiches were gone. Bella took out another one. And then another. Two sandwiches would be okay for Mason. He'd probably already had lunch.

The minutes passed. There was no sign of Mason. Bella whistled her favorite sailing song. The wind carried away her tune the moment it left her lips. It was really starting to blow hard. And the surf seemed louder, too.

Bella counted the waves. She was up to three when she heard a new sound, faint above the rest. A voice was calling her name! Bella stood up and prepared to run. Maybe Salty was mad at her for breaking into his house!

"Up here," the voice said.

He was flying down to get her! Bella looked up and saw something flapping at the top of the tower. It was not a ghost. It was Mason waving his hat.

"I've got a sandwich for you!" Bella waved back. She hoped it would hurry him along.

When Mason finally came out, Bella was just polishing off the fifth sandwich. "Here." She offered him the bag. "My mom's a great cook."

"I couldn't possibly eat now," Mason said. His eyes were as bright as a shooting star. He hurried ahead of Bella down the path. He was moving fast. Bella could barely cram the last sandwich in her mouth as she trotted along behind him. He was definitely on edge. Was he upset about the ghost? Bella couldn't tell.

Bella stole a last look at the lighthouse over her shoulder. And stopped in her tracks. On the widow's walk—the part of the lighthouse that surrounded the light—she thought she saw a person. She stared at the spot for a long moment. But she did not see the figure again. The fog was playing tricks with her eyes.

Shivering, she ran to catch up. Mason was talk-

ing now—a mile a minute. "A whole new angle," he said. "We'll have to use a whole new angle."

Bella wondered if that was because of the ghost. Or because of the damage her dad had done to the camera holder.

"Bella, your ghost will give this film new life!" Mason whirled around.

*Her* ghost? Bella didn't want Salty to be *her* ghost. She was actually hoping he would leave her alone. But she loved that Mason was giving her credit for an idea he was so excited about.

"We can shoot everything right here in Sandyport," Mason went on. "I even have a new title in mind: *Salty Spirit: The Haunting of the Sandyport Lighthouse.*"

Bella shivered again. Mason saw and grinned. "It's good, huh?"

Bella returned his smile. But she had chills for a different reason. "The inn is just down this path and then four more blocks. Do you think you can make it back by yourself?" Bella asked.

Mason nodded and Bella waved. Then she

dashed off in the other direction, toward town. As anxious as she was to be back in her cozy home, Bella needed to make one more stop.

"It was so . . . eerie." Bella leaned over the information desk. She was just finishing telling Trudy everything. "He was there. I'm sure of it."

Trudy nodded gravely and pointed at the weather section of the newspaper. "I don't doubt it. Salty stays away, sometimes for months on end. But he always comes back when there's a really big storm brewing." She leaned forward and peered at Bella over her half-glasses. "And there's one brewing now."

CHAPTER 7

# Gloomy Day

The sky outside Bella's window was gray. Not misty, foggy gray like the day before. This gray was the gray of gathering clouds. This gray looked like rain and thunder. But it did nothing to dampen Bella's mood. She felt great. More important, Bella felt brave.

Maybe it was the great dream she'd just had. She'd been a lighthouse keeper. She'd shone great beams of light out to sea and saved sailors. Or maybe it was the way Trudy's eyes had lit up when Bella told her about seeing Salty through the fog. Either way, Bella had realized something.

What lay before her was a new adventure. And all of the parts of her that had been scared before were now ready for action.

Bella searched through a dresser drawer. She shoved her bright colored clothes aside. She pulled on a black turtleneck and jeans. She braided her thick brown hair and tied a bandanna over it, like Darla did. There. She looked just like one of the crew.

"I'm going back to the lighthouse today," Bella announced as she walked into the kitchen. "With Mason," she added when her parents made no reply. "And the crew."

Nellie was standing by her husband at the kitchen table. Barnaby was slumped in a chair. He didn't look well. "Are they taking the equipment?" Barnaby asked.

"I hope so," Bella's mom mumbled. She patted Barnaby gently on the shoulder.

Bella stared at her dad. He had a bruise on his arm and another on his forehead. And he was wearing sunglasses.

"Daddy, what happened?" Bella asked. "You don't look so great."

"I was trying to figure out how all this equipment works. The crew was helping me, even. But I guess I'm just not cut out for this Hollywood stuff." Barnaby sighed sadly.

"You should have seen him, Bell." Nellie shook her head. But Bella could tell her smile was not far away. "He talked them into making a whole mini-set right out there on the porch."

"I didn't know those lights were so bright. You

should never look right into them, BB." He gave his eyes a serious rub under his glasses. "And now I know why they call those big overhead microphones 'booms.'" Barnaby's hand drifted up to his bruised forehead. He smiled weakly. "I think today I'll just do some work in the garden."

"Good idea." Bella's mom winked.

Soon the breakfast dishes were cleared, and Bella was ready to go. She tried to read some more of her lighthouse books while she waited for everyone else to get ready. But she was too excited to focus. The words kept jumping all around. Finally the crew was set to go, and they were out the door.

"I didn't know we'd hired more help," Lyle joked. "What are you, key grip or best boy?"

"Key girl," Bella said. Everyone laughed. Bella made a mental note to ask Trudy about key grips and best boys later. She had seen them listed in movie credits, of course. But she had no idea what they did.

Though the day was dark and windy, Bella could see the lighthouse long before they got to it. She squinted toward the tower. There was nobody there except a couple of seagulls.

The board was still across the door, but Bella did not hesitate. She ducked right under. "Who wants to climb the tower?" she asked.

Darla and Sterling set down their heavy duffels to follow. Lyle left his outside.

Smiling to herself, Bella led them through the tiny cottage. Everything seemed just the same as yesterday. Only *she* felt different. Then Bella noticed something else that was different.

The teacup and teakettle were gone.

Bella shivered. *Maybe Mason put them away yesterday,* she thought. She opened the little door to the winding stairs. "It's dark in here, but you don't have to be afraid," she told the crew. Bella felt her way up to the first landing. Then a noise made her turn around. There was a new voice in the cottage. Somebody was talking to Mason—Trudy!

Bella ran back down the stairs. She had to introduce her old friend to her new friends! She'd had a feeling Trudy might show up here. But she hadn't thought she'd be so early!

"Mason, this is Trudy. She knows everything about everything. Trudy, this is Mason Hawk. He's the best documentary filmmaker ever."

Trudy waggled a finger but could not shake hands. Her arms were full of old books and papers and a large white bag.

"I don't know if I'm the *best* documentary film-maker." Mason blushed.

"Well, I am sure I don't know everything about everything. But I do know where to find out." Trudy set her stack of books and papers on the table. She wiped her hands on her fisher-man's sweater. "These are the lighthouse records dating back thirty-five years. I got them at the historical society."

Mason looked impressed.

"And I also know where to get great pastries." Trudy grinned at Bella and held up the white bag.

"Bruno's!" Bella shouted.

Trudy separated her stacks while everyone gathered around. "These are Salty's own records." Trudy thumped a stack of leather-bound ledgers. "These are reported lighthouse light sightings in the ten years since Salty disappeared," Trudy said. There was a note of mystery in her voice. "This is the nautical weather log for the Connecticut coast." Trudy pulled a croissant out of the white bag. "And *these* are the best croissants this side of the Atlantic."

"Where did you find her?" Mason whispered to Bella. He helped himself to a croissant. Then he sat down to look at the ledgers.

"At my local library," Bella whispered back. She leaned in for a closer look at the ledgers herself. Salty's handwriting was long and skinny and not very neat. The pages were covered with ring-shaped stains. *Tea rings,* Bella thought.

Bella picked up one of the sailors' reports. It was a letter addressed to the *Sandyport Tribune.*

*I thought we were done for. The storm was pounding*

*on the hull. Our radio and sonar had shorted out. I knew
we were close to shore, but how close I could not tell. In
the rain and fog and huge swells I could not see a thing
until a light shone from the old lighthouse. I had not seen
that old light in years, not since I was a child out with
my dad. But it never looked so beautiful as it did that
night.*

*The spirit of Salty Dobin saved another ship, and
another life.*

Bella shivered and put the paper down. Was
Salty's ghost really saving the lives of local
sailors? She wasn't sure. But she was sure of
something else: Salty's story was going to make
a great movie!

While Trudy and Mason talked, Bella grabbed
a pair of old binoculars off the wall. She started
up the tower steps yet again. She was determined
to make it to the top this time. She climbed and
climbed and finally saw the gray light of day. She
pushed her way outside, and she squinted into
the wind. She could see forever!

Bending over the rail, Bella looked down. The

rocks on the beach looked like pebbles. Even the houses in town looked like toys. Bella held the binoculars up to her face. She gazed in the direction of her house. There it was! There was Sea Inn! She could practically look inside her own bedroom. Bella watched for a while, trying to see her mom or dad. Then she let the binoculars hang around her neck. She stared out at the churning sea.

The waves were huge in the wind. They were pounding the beach and rocks. They sent up spray and left white foam on the sand. Suddenly something caught Bella's eye. A tiny dark form was moving on the rocks in front of the lighthouse. It looked like a person.

Through the binoculars, Bella saw something else. The figure was wearing a blue sailor's cap just like the one she'd seen on Salty's wall.

# CHAPTER 8

# Friend or Foe?

"Salty?" Bella gasped. She steadied her hands and focused the binoculars a little better. No. The person below her was way too young to be Salty. He looked like a boy, about eight, her age. And he was coming closer and closer to the lighthouse.

The boy was almost to the door. He stopped and crouched beside the big bag Lyle had leaned against the wall. He looked over his shoulder and reached for the zipper.

"Hey!" Bella yelled. She dropped the binoculars so they hung around her neck again. "Hey, what are you doing?" The boy looked up at her. But he did not take his hands off the bag. Had he heard her? The surf was so loud there was no way to know.

Bella turned and ran as fast as she could down the dark stairs. Trudy and Mason looked up as Bella streaked by them. A second later she was out the door.

"Hey," Bella said again, breathlessly. "Who are you? What are you doing here? Are you spying on us?"

The boy did not look surprised to see Bella. He only looked grumpy.

"You're the one with binoculars," he pointed out coolly. "You're the one who looks like you're spying. And you're trespassing."

Bella looked at the binoculars hanging around her neck. She looked at the DO NOT ENTER sign behind her back. He had a point.

Bella ignored the boy's scowl. She stuck out her hand. "I'm Bella," she said. She did not want to get off on the wrong foot and get Mason in

trouble. "I'm here making a movie about this old lighthouse."

"You're making a movie?" The boy looked curious. But Bella could tell he did not believe her.

"Well, I'm here with Mason Hawk. He's making the movie. I'm sort of his assistant. Actually, I'm the expert on this lighthouse—and the ghost that haunts it."

"You mean Salty." The boy snorted. "Everybody knows about Salty. What makes you such an expert?"

"I've read at least ten books about lighthouses, and I've seen Salty's records." Bella started to defend herself. She was trying to be nice, but he wasn't making it easy.

"I bet I'm more of an expert than you. Read all you want. You can't beat living here. I know all of Salty's secrets. I bet you don't even know how to turn on the big light." The boy crossed his arms and looked at Bella defiantly.

"You live here?" Bella could not help being impressed. "Really?"

"Well, I stayed the night," the boy admitted. "And I did turn on the light. But it was an accident."

"Wow." Bella was almost speechless.

"Yeah." The boy nodded. "It was really cool. I'm Jonas." He finally stuck out his hand. Bella shook it.

"Was it scary to stay here at night?" Bella asked. "Did you see Salty?"

Jonas laughed. "Salty's been gone for years, but it *was* kind of scary to stay here. My brother came too. And we had flashlights and stuff," Jonas admitted. "Mostly we stayed up telling stories."

Well, that explained a lot. Like the teakettle and the footsteps.

"I found a secret room," Jonas went on.

"You did? Where?" Bella asked. Jonas was turning out to be pretty cool after all!

"I'll show you." Jonas ducked under the board. "Don't worry about the sign. My uncle owns this place. He just put it there to keep kids out."

"Like us?" Bella laughed.

"Hi, Jonas," Trudy said as Jonas led Bella past the table to the bedroom.

"Hi," Jonas said back.

"You know Trudy?" Bella knew she shouldn't be surprised. After all, she had just introduced Trudy as a person who knew everything. But she couldn't help being a little bit jealous.

"Sure." Jonas shrugged. "She helped me and my uncle build a Japanese fishpond in our backyard. Here it is." Jonas pulled a knothole in the wall. A small door, smaller than the one to the lighthouse stairs, swung open. Behind it was a long, narrow room. It was filled with even more ship parts.

Bella stepped inside and let her eyes adjust to the dim light. She shuffled toward the back, looking at the rusty riggings and pulleys. There were even some big bones that must have belonged to a whale.

"I found an old compass in here. And there's a spyglass, too. I bet it works as good as your binoculars." Jonas poked around on a small shelf.

Bella shuffled farther toward the back of the murky room. She stepped on a loose floorboard. Her foot slipped into the gap and her pants caught. "Ouch."

"Are you okay?" Jonas asked.

"Yeah," Bella replied. She bent down to tug her pant leg free. The whole board came with it. "But I think I found something else!"

# CHAPTER 9

# Dusty Discoveries

Jonas was kneeling on the floor next to Bella in a second. The two peered into the hole. It was dark and smelled a little musty. Bella could just make out a squarish shape.

"What is it?" Jonas asked.

"Not sure," Bella replied. "I think it's a box." She reached inside and pulled out an old wooden crate. It was full of dusty letters and a faded leather-bound book.

Jonas's eyebrows shot up. "Whoa," he said.

Bella wiped the dust off the book—"Achoo!" There was so much dust, it made her sneeze. But she didn't care. She felt like a detective who had just found the final clue. The clue that would solve the case.

Suddenly the little door to the secret room slammed closed. Bella jumped. The room was really dark now. Bella couldn't even make out the letters on the front of the book in her lap.

Jonas got up and opened the door. Some light came back in. Jonas sat back down in front of the crate of letters.

JOURNAL. That's what the book said. Bella opened it up. She recognized Salty's long, skinny handwriting right away. Bella began to read the words. It was kind of tricky, but she got the hang of it pretty fast.

"Jonas, listen to this!" she cried after a few minutes.

Jonas looked up from the pile of old letters in the crate.

"'I love the solitude of my lighthouse and the freedom to come and go when I wish. But that last storm came so quickly, I almost didn't make it. A close call for an old sailor. Someday I won't be so lucky.'"

"Wow!" Jonas said. "Is there a date?"

Bella looked in the corner of the page. There was a date, but it was covered by a ring-shaped stain. Just like the stains on the log.

"There is, but it's covered up," Bella said. She squinted in the dim light. "I think it's a $J$ month in 1991."

Bella turned the page and kept reading. She couldn't believe she was reading Salty Dobin's personal journal! Jonas sifted through the pile of letters. There were a lot of them. Most had handwritten addresses: Elijah Dobin, The Sandyport Lighthouse, Sandyport, Connecticut, 06842. But there was one near the bottom of the pile that had a typed address and an official-looking seal. It was from the United States government, from the Office of Nautical Regulation and Safety.

"Look at this!" Jonas said as he opened the envelope. He unfolded the thick, faded paper and began to read:

Dear Mr. Dobin,

It is with regret that we inform you that your position as lighthouse keeper in the lighthouse of Sandyport, Connecticut, shall be eliminated as of June 1, 1993, and the lighthouse shall be closed. Sonar technology has made it safe for ships to pass through that particular area without lighthouse assistance. As a result we will no longer be needing your lighthouse keeper services.

Thank you for your many years of faithful lighthouse operation.

Regards,

William C. Landho

Office of Nautical Regulation and Safety

Jonas dropped the letter to his lap. "Poor Salty! They fired him and closed down his lighthouse!"

Bella was only half listening. She'd turned a few more pages in the journal. She was reading another entry.

Those fools claim that they are closing my lighthouse. But they cannot take it from me. I belong here, by the sea. This shall be my home for the rest of my days. And I shall continue to light the way.

Bella got tingly all over as she read Salty's words.

"I can't believe they took the lighthouse away from him!" Jonas said. He sounded mad.

Bella raised an eyebrow at her new friend. "They *tried* to take the lighthouse away from him," she said. She read the entry to Jonas. By the time she was finished, Jonas was on his feet.

"Come on!" he said. "We've got to show this stuff to Mr. Hawk and Trudy!"

# CHAPTER 10

# Salty's Return

Bella and Jonas were both out of breath by the time they got to the living quarters. Mason and Trudy were still sitting at the table sifting through the lighthouse records. Trudy had marked a bunch of pages with her Post-its. Mason had jotted down some notes on a separate pad.

"They tried to fire him!" Jonas panted.

"But old Salty wouldn't give in! He still comes back to the lighthouse!" Bella practically shouted.

"Hold up there, kiddos," Trudy said. "And start again from the beginning."

"You go first," Bella said. She pointed to the letter in Jonas's hand. Jonas read the letter, and then Bella read Salty's response in his journal. Mason listened closely, his eyes thoughtful.

As soon as they finished, Trudy started flipping through the weather log. Bella could tell she was on to something.

It took Trudy a few minutes to find what she was looking for. When she did, her eyebrows shot up above the tops of her glasses.

"It seems Salty was coming and going for a lot longer than we thought," she said. "After his 'disappearance' in the early nineties, he returned whenever a really big storm was brewing. The storms listed in the weather log match up with the sailors' light sightings."

"Sonar or no sonar, Salty had to light the way," Bella said.

Trudy nodded. "Yup," she agreed. "At least until Hurricane Hubert. That's when the sightings come to a screeching halt."

Everyone was silent as the meaning of Trudy's

words sunk in. Hurricane Hubert was the biggest hurricane the Atlantic Coast had seen in decades. It had hit just last year. And Trudy was right. The lighthouse light hadn't been lit since. Except for the time Jonas turned it on by accident.

"Salty was swallowed by the sea, just like he'd predicted," Bella said. She read the entry about the close call to everyone at the table.

Trudy patted Bella on the arm. "Don't feel bad, Bell," she said. "A true sailor like Salty would have been proud to give his life to the sea."

Bella sighed. She knew Trudy was right, but she felt sad just the same. Sad that Salty was gone. And a little disappointed that the ghost legend wasn't true after all.

Mason cleared his throat. Bella suddenly realized that he'd been awfully quiet.

"Looks like I'll be changing my documentary *again*," he said. "And I'll be needing some new talent. Some fresh, new, young talent. Know any kids who might be interested in narrating a story? It's about a Connecticut lighthouse and

Salty the sailor. There won't be a ghost, but I'm pretty sure we can still make it mysterious."

Bella blinked. Was he saying what she thought he was saying? The grin on his face told her he was.

"I could never have learned so much about Salty if it wasn't for your discovery. How would you two like to narrate the film?"

Bella grabbed on to Jonas's arm. The two of them jumped up and down. "We would!" she squealed. "We absolutely, positively would!"

"This calls for a celebration!" Trudy announced. She pulled out a thermos and another bag from Bruno's. "Hot tea and cookies, anyone?"

Jonas peeked inside the white paper bag and grinned. "I'd love a cookie," he said. "But no tea for me. I can't stand the stuff."

Bella stared at her new friend. "Didn't you leave a teakettle and a teacup on the table yesterday?" she asked. She suddenly felt a little spooked.

Jonas shook his head. "Nope. I really don't like tea."

Heavy footsteps sounded on the floor above them.

Trudy raised an eyebrow. "Didn't you send your crew back to the inn?" she asked Mason.

Mason nodded.

Everyone at the table looked up at the ceiling. The footsteps sounded again.

Bella shivered and took a sip of tea. "Welcome back, Salty!" she called loudly.

There was a moment of silence. Then the wind gusted and the door to the lighthouse stairs slammed shut.

"I think that means 'Thank you,'" Jonas said.

Everyone at the table nodded in agreement. Then Bella held up her cookie in a toast. "To Salty," she said.

"To Salty," everyone chorused. And they all clinked chocolate chips.